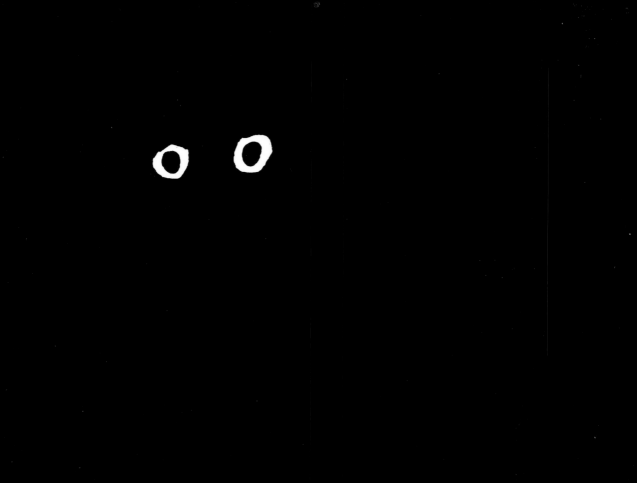

Life is good.
I am Milton.

Anyway, I take my
meals in the kitchen.
My bowl is always full.

...when I care to give chase.

I am an excellent hunter...

Hello, little mouse.

Nothing escapes me.

I am fearless.

My days are very busy.

and expressive ears.

This means: Do not come one step closer.

and retractable claws —

very sharp

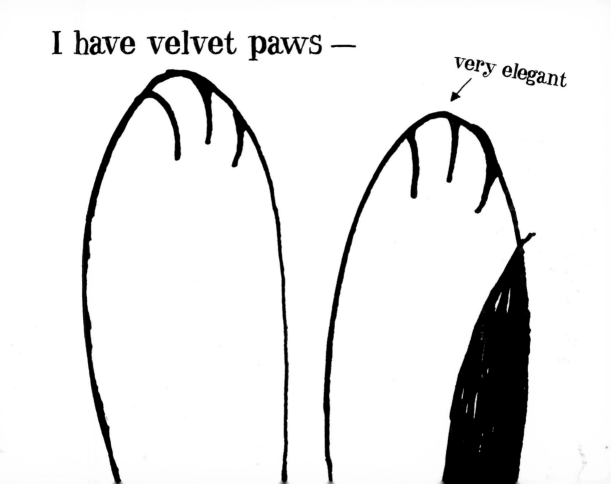

I see everything,
day or night.

There:
an even better smell

Here:
a good smell

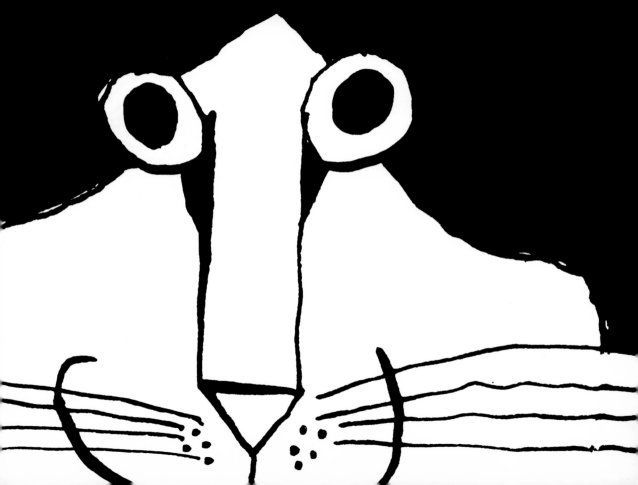

I am
extremely
handsome
and I have
a curious
nose.

I am an exceptional cat.

Now I am big.
My name is Milton.

Once I was little.

Milton

Haydé Ardalan

chronicle books · san francisco

Milton
2nd printing
copyright page corrections

Distributed in Canada by Raincoast Books
9050 Shaughnessy Street
Vancouver, British Columbia V6P 6E5

10 9 8 7 6 5 4 3 2

Chronicle Books LLC
85 Second Street
San Francisco, California 94105

www.chroniclebooks.com

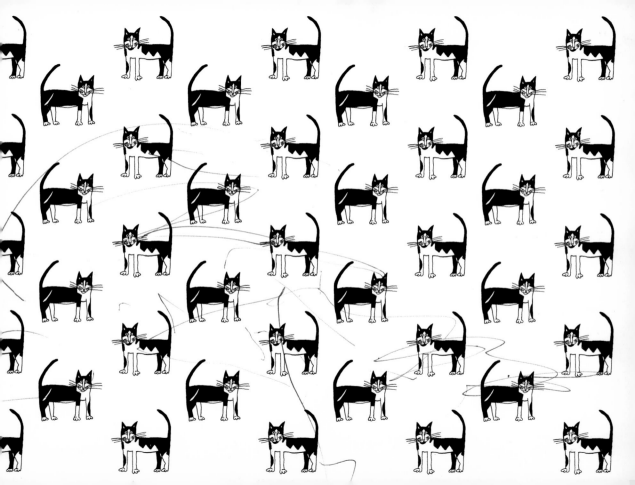